GRANDPA CHATTERJI

EGMONT PRESS: ETHICAL PUBLISHING

Egmont Press is about turning writers into successful authors and children into passionate readers – producing books that enrich and entertain. As a responsible children's publisher, we go even further, considering the world in which our consumers are growing up.

Safety First
Naturally, all of our books meet legal safety requirements. But we go further than this; every book with play value is tested to the highest standards – if it fails, it's back to the drawing-board.

Made Fairly
We are working to ensure that the workers involved in our supply chain – the people that make our books – are treated with fairness and respect.

Responsible Forestry
We are committed to ensuring all our papers come from environmentally and socially responsible forest sources.

For more information, please visit our website at
www.egmont.co.uk/ethicalpublishing

Jamila Gavin

GRANDPA CHATTERJI

Illustrated by Peter Bailey

EGMONT

Ask a grown-up to help you with the recipe at the back.

EGMONT
We bring stories to life

First published in Great Britain 1993
by Egmont UK Limited
239 Kensington High Street
London W8 6SA

This edition published 2006

Text copyright © 1993 Jamila Gavin
Illustrations © 2006 Peter Bailey

The moral rights of the author and illustrator have been asserted

ISBN 978 1 4052 1285 4

3 5 7 9 10 8 6 4

A CIP catalogue record for this title is available from the British Library

Printed and bound in Great Britain by the CPI Group

Contents

'What are you doing, Grandpa?'

Neetu and her little brother Sanjay have two grandpas – Mum's dad and Dad's dad.

Mum's dad lives in India and they have never ever seen him. But Dad's dad lives in Leicester and they see him quite often.

Although they love and respect Dad's

dad, as head of the family, Neetu and Sanjay are a little afraid of him. Whenever he comes to visit, they all have to be on their toes.

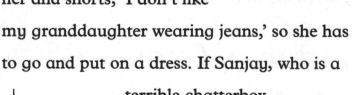

If Neetu wears jeans, Grandpa Leicester frowns at her and snorts, 'I don't like my granddaughter wearing jeans,' so she has to go and put on a dress. If Sanjay, who is a

terrible chatterbox, sometimes interrupts, Grandfather glares at him sternly and says, 'I don't like little boys who interrupt,' and Sanjay has to bite his lip and try so hard not to speak.

When their mother got a

job and went out to work, Grandfather was very disapproving. 'I don't like my daughter-in-law going out to work.' Mum just smiled politely, and went anyway, and Dad took his father aside to try to explain how with Mum going to work, they could afford a new car.

Perhaps the worst time is when Dad's dad comes to stay and they can't eat their favourite pizza and chips. Instead, they have to eat vegetable curry, runny spinach with eggs, and horrible stuff like that.

One day, Mum said excitedly, 'Children! Your grandpa is coming to stay! Isn't that wonderful!' But they didn't think it was wonderful at all. Neetu just groaned and said, 'Oh no! I'll have to wear nothing but dresses,' and Sanjay moaned, 'Oh no! We'll have to eat curried eggs.'

It was Dad who beamed at them and said, 'It's not my dad from Leicester who's coming to visit us, it's your mum's dad from Calcutta. You've never met him! You can call him "Grandpa Chatterji".'

Neetu and Sanjay looked at each other doubtfully. How could they know whether a grandad from Calcutta was any different from a grandad from Leicester, even if he was called Grandpa Chatterji? They would just have to wait and see.

All that week Mum went round with a smile on her face, and even Dad seemed quite relaxed. Mum got the spare room ready, just as she always did for Dad's dad. But instead of worriedly scrubbing and cleaning and polishing and checking that there was not one speck of dust to be seen anywhere in the house, she actually hummed and sang and seemed to enjoy making everything look nice.

On the day of his arrival, Mum and Dad got up very early and drove off to the airport to meet Grandpa Chatterji. Neetu and Sanjay didn't go because there wouldn't be room in the car on the way back. Old Mrs Bennet from next door came in to look after them.

They waited and waited. Sanjay looked out of one window and Neetu looked out of

the other. What would he be like? Would he wear a smart suit and shiny black shoes like Dad's dad? Would he smoke cigars and sit in the best easy chair and talk business with Dad in a big boomy voice? Would he have the best bed? Would he be served first at table? Would he always insist on using the bathroom first in the morning, even though he took the longest and made them late for school? And would he be critical and strict and insist on total obedience at all times?

They waited and waited. Suddenly, Sanjay shouted, 'They're here!' The little red Mini had pulled up outside the house.

'Oh dear,' cried Neetu, suddenly going all shy, 'I'm going to hide.'

They both hid behind the sofa. They heard the front door open. They heard Mum come in and say gently, 'Welcome to our home!' They heard Dad say, 'I'll take your luggage up to your room,' and they heard a thin, quiet, soft voice say, 'And where are my little grandchildren?'

Then there was silence. Crouched behind the sofa, Neetu and Sanjay hardly breathed. Then suddenly, although they didn't hear Grandpa Chatterji come into the room, they knew he was there because they saw a pair of bare, dark-brown, knobbly, long-toed, bony feet.

The feet came and stood right close by them. The feet emerged from beneath thin, white trousers and, as their eyes travelled all the way up, past a white tunic and brown waistcoat and past a red and blue woolly scarf round the neck, they found themselves looking into a round, shining, kind, wrinkly face, with deep-as-oceans large, brown eyes, and a mass of pure, white, fluffy hair which fell in a tangle over his brow.

'Ah!' exclaimed Grandpa Chatterji with a great, loving sigh, and he opened his arms to embrace them.

After they had all hugged each other, Mum said, 'Children, take Grandpa up to his room, he will want to bath and change after his long journey. I'll go and make a nice cup of tea.'

Sanjay began chattering as he clambered up the stairs, leading the way.

'Why aren't you wearing any shoes?' he asked.

'Because I took them off at the door, so as not to bring any dirt into the house. We always do that in India,' answered Grandpa Chatterji.

'Did you come with lots of suitcases, Grandpa?' Sanjay went on, 'and did you bring us lots of presents?'

'Ssh!' said Neetu, embarrassed. 'That's rude, Sanjay.'

'Just you wait and see,' replied Grandpa, who didn't mind at all.

When they went into the guest room, they couldn't see any suitcases at all.

'Where is your luggage?' asked Neetu.

'Oh, I only ever travel with my bedroll,' said Grandpa. 'My needs are very simple,' and he pointed to a roly-poly round khaki canvas roll, all held together with leather straps, and covered in airline stickers and labels.

'Does that mean we don't have presents?' sighed Sanjay.

'Just you wait and see,' replied Grandpa again.

'You've got the best room in the house,' chattered Sanjay, bravely trying to ignore the mysterious roll which contained everything that Grandpa had brought.

'You've got the nicest sheets with duvet and curtains to match, you have the plumpiest pillows and the softest bed. It's the best bed in the house for bouncing on,' and Sanjay flung himself on to the bed, which

Mum had made all smooth and neat, and he rumpled it all up.

'Sanjay!' cried Neetu with horror, dragging him off. 'Look what you've done,' and she tried to straighten it out.

'If you like this bed so much, you'd better sleep in it,' said Grandpa Chatterji. 'I prefer something harder.'

'Where will you sleep then, Grandpa?' asked Neetu looking worried.

'I'll sleep on the floor as I always do,' he replied. 'I am like a snail, my dear,' murmured Grandpa. 'All I need, wherever I

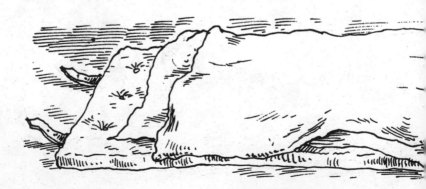

go, is my bedroll. It carries all my belongings, and when I unroll it, it becomes my bed.'

The children looked in awe at the khaki, canvas roll. It suddenly seemed to be the most important thing in the world. 'Can we unroll it, Grandpa?' whispered Sanjay.

Grandpa bent over the roll and undid the old leather straps, then he slowly unrolled it alongside the bed. At first it seemed that all it contained was one sheet and one blanket. Sanjay was sure there were no presents; but then Grandpa wriggled his hand into the

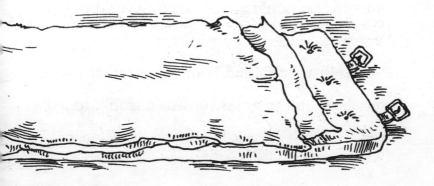

large pocket at one end of the roll and pulled

out a tooth mug and toothbrush all wrapped

in a towel, a hair brush and

comb and his shaving things.

Sanjay stared expectantly.

Were there any

presents?

Then Grandpa went

to a pocket at the other

end and wriggled his

hand inside. He pulled

out a woolly jumper, a

woolly hat, some socks,

underwear, hankies, a shirt, tunic and

waistcoat, but still no presents.

At last, he folded back the sheet. Between

the sheet and the blanket was a small, faded

rug. He pulled back the rug to show lots of

different packages.

'Presents!' breathed Sanjay, full of expectation.

'Why did you bring that old rug?' asked Neetu in a puzzled voice.

Grandpa Chatterji lifted it out as though it were the most precious thing in the world. 'I never go anywhere without this,' he murmured. 'It is my meditation rug. I sit on it to do all my thinking and praying.'

'Are those things presents?' asked Sanjay, pointing to the packages.

'Yes, yes, here you are,' laughed Grandpa. He handed Sanjay two long thin packages.

'Thank you, thank you!' yelled Sanjay, ripping them open. 'What are they?'

'One is a specially made, wooden wriggly

snake, and the other is an Indian flute. Later
I will teach you some tunes, but for now, you
can just blow. It makes a lovely sound.
Snakes love the sound of the flute. It
makes them sway and
puts them into a good
mood.'

Sanjay flung his
arms round his old
grandfather. 'Thank
you, thank you,
Grandpa Chatterji!' and he rushed off
to show his mum and dad.

Neetu waited patiently. Which package
was for her? He bent over and handed her
one of the larger ones. 'What a beauty you
are, my dearest little granddaughter! This is
for you.'

When Neetu opened up
her package, she found a
beautiful pink and green and
gold sari. It was a special
small-sized sari for little girls.
In India they have to wait
until they are nearly grown-
up before they can wear a
sari, but all little girls love to
have a sari they can dress up
in, and this is what her
grandfather had brought for
her.

It made Neetu feel very
solemn and proud. 'Oh thank
you, Grandpa!' she declared
in a grown-up voice, 'I'll
go and ask Mum to help

me put it on.'

Later, when Grandpa Chatterji had bathed and changed, Neetu, all dressed up in her sari, and Sanjay, with his snake and flute, went upstairs to find him. They knocked on his door.

'Come in!' he said in his soft, high voice.

They went in. Grandpa was sitting on the floor on his old rug. He was sitting very straight, his eyes staring in front and his arms stretched over his cross-legged knees.

'What are you doing, Grandpa?' asked Sanjay.

'I'm being a lotus flower floating quietly on a sea of milk.'

'Why are you being a lotus flower?' asked Neetu. She was looking like such a beautiful, grown-up lady in her new sari.

Grandpa looked at her and smiled with admiration. 'Come, children. Come and sit next to me. There's room on the rug.'

Neetu and Sanjay sat cross-legged one on each side of their grandfather. They stretched out their arms over their knees and straightened their backs.

'We are being lotus flowers because we are trying to be as calm and peaceful and perfect as lotus flowers are,' explained Grandpa Chatterji, 'and if you close your eyes, you can imagine you are floating on a sea of milk before the creation of the world.'

The children closed their eyes and floated away.

Then Grandpa suddenly woke up with a shout and cried, 'I feel rested now! Come on! Where's that cup of tea your mother promised me? And while I'm drinking my tea, Sanjay can play the flute, and Neetu can dance! Will you?' he begged, his dark eyes glittering.

Neetu and Sanjay nodded with excitement. 'Oh, Grandpa Chatterji! We're so glad you came.'

'Ōm … Ōm … Ōm …'

When Neetu awoke the next morning, the
first thing she thought was, 'Did Grandpa
Chatterji really sleep on the floor?'

She sat up wide awake. It must be very
early, because her room was still dark. Just a
faint grey streak of light slipped between the
curtains. Outside, the first blackbird had
begun his dawn song.

She crept along to Grandpa Chatterji's
room. His door was open. She peeped inside.
At first she couldn't see anything. Then as
her eyes adjusted, she saw that the spare bed,
with its flowery duvet, was empty and hadn't
been touched. On the floor, rolled out with a
flat pillow and blanket was Grandpa
Chatterji's bedroll; but there was no sign of
Grandpa. Then she heard the sound. A slow,
low repeating sound like the throbbing of a
fridge, or the wind

strumming the telephone wire. Or was it? Neetu listened carefully. Was it her own heart beating? No. Her heart was going boom, boom, boom, like a softly muffled drum. This sound was more like the waves beating against the shore; or a giant breathing . . . or . . .?

Ōm . . . Ōm . . . Ōm . . . The sound seemed to be everywhere; inside and outside. Was it Sanjay playing his flute? She tiptoed out of her bedroom and looked

into her brother's room. He lay fast asleep,
sprawled across his bed with his feet sticking
out, and an arm flung over his best teddy.
His wooden flute lay waiting patiently upon
his pillow. Sanjay wasn't making the sound.
Was it Dad snoring? She crept into her
parents' bedroom. She saw their two humps
side by side like bookends under the double
duvet. She went closer and stood listening.
But no, Mum and Dad were still so deeply
asleep that you could hardly hear them
breathing at all.

So she went downstairs, past the ticking clock in the hall, past the puff of the boiler as it fired the central heating, past the low throbbing of the fridge and up to the back door. Here, the sound seemed louder. It was coming from the garden. Ōm . . . Ōm . . . Ŏm . . . Was it the tree moaning in the wind?

She went outside. It wasn't a very big garden. Just a patch of lawn with two long flower beds running the length of the fence on each side. The best thing was the tree at the bottom. It wasn't the sort of tree anyone would plant. Its seed had been blown there by the wind long before Neetu was even born. It had grown quietly and secretly without anybody noticing. It had grown and grown till it was taller than their house. Its branches stretched out like lots of arms, and

sometimes the wind blew around it, making it creak and swish. It was where the blackbird sang his songs and where the sparrows caused kerfuffles among the clumps of ivy which clung to the trunk. But as Neetu stood outside the back door, she realised that it was a perfectly still morning, with not one breath of wind to even rustle the leaves. Ōm . . . Ōm . . . Ōm . . .

Then she saw him. Grandpa Chatterji was standing at the base of the tree. He wasn't wearing stripy pyjamas as Grandpa Leicester always did. He was bare-footed and was only wearing a thin white cloth wrapped round his waist and a white thread across his bare chest. He had spread out his precious

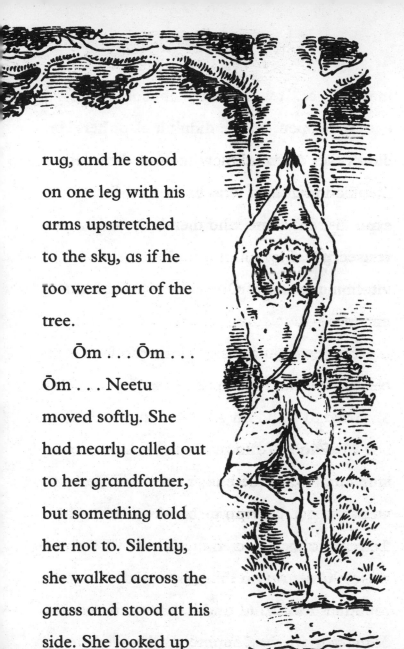

rug, and he stood
on one leg with his
arms upstretched
to the sky, as if he
too were part of the
tree.

 Ōm . . . Ōm . . .
Ōm . . . Neetu
moved softly. She
had nearly called out
to her grandfather,
but something told
her not to. Silently,
she walked across the
grass and stood at his
side. She looked up

into his face. It was completely calm. His eyes were open, but he didn't look at her. He didn't even seem to know she was there. He breathed in a long, long breath which expanded his chest, and then he breathed out very very slowly. As he did, the deep, throbbing sound of Ōm soared through the air.

There was just room on the rug for Neetu. Without asking, she stood by his side. She tried to stand on one leg, but wobbled. She tried again, and managed to stand for a little longer. She raised her arms and looked up at the sky. Dawn was breaking through the grey branches, creating islands of pink clouds. Ōm . . . Ōm . . . She copied.

After a while, Grandpa Chatterji looked down at his granddaughter and smiled.

'What are we doing, Grandpa?' she whispered.

'We're praying to God and welcoming a new day. When you make a round shape with your lips and say "O" you are making the shape of the sun, the shape of the world and the shape of the universe. When you make the sound "Ōm" you are talking to the Creator of Everything.'

Then suddenly, Grandpa stopped being holy.

'I'm starving!' he cried. 'Let's make *pooris*!' He seemed to fly down the garden and into the kitchen. Neetu had to run to keep up.

'Where's the flour?' he asked.

Neetu found the flour.

'Where's the cooking oil?'

Neetu found the cooking oil.

'Where's the mixing bowl?'

Neetu found the mixing bowl.

'Where's the rolling pin?'

Neetu found the rolling pin.

Then Grandpa Chatterji put down his rug on the floor in a corner of the kitchen and began to mix the dough.

Sanjay came in playing his flute. He was still in his pyjamas and his eyes were sticky with sleep.

'Where have you been? I was looking everywhere for you,' he grumbled.

'Grandpa and I were saying hello to the

sun,' explained Neetu. 'Look! We stood like this.'

Neetu stood on one leg with her arms up above her head. She breathed in deeply, and as she breathed out, she went 'Ōm . . .'

'That's easy!' scoffed Sanjay. 'I can do that!' But when he tried, he wobbled all over the place.

'Come and help me with the *pooris*, you two!' interrupted Grandpa. 'Look! I've kneaded the dough. Now you take a handful and work it round into a ball. Then flatten it out on this wooden board and roll it into a circle with the rolling pin. I'll heat up the cooking oil.'

When the oil was smoking hot, one by one, Grandpa dropped the rolled-out circles of dough into the sizzling pan.

'Look!' cried Neetu excitedly. 'Look how they puff up!'

'They're just like little footballs!' yelled Sanjay.

'They're round like Ōm,' said Neetu.

Soon they had a plate piled high with *pooris*.

Grandpa had boiled a kettle and made a big pot of tea. He said, 'Let's take your mother and father tea and *pooris* in bed!'

Neetu and Sanjay carried a plate each of *pooris* while Grandpa put five mugs of steaming hot tea on the tray. Then in procession, they climbed the stairs.

Mum and Dad sat up in amazement

when they all trooped into the bedroom.

'*Garam Chai*!' announced Grandpa.
'Hot tea!'

'And *pooris* which we made!' boasted
Sanjay.

'It's just like being back in India,' sighed
Mum.

'These were always your mum's favourite
when she was a little girl,' smiled Grandpa
Chatterji.

'I think they're my favourite too,'
cried Neetu with her mouth full.

Sanjay stood on one leg.
He put his hands up above
his head and, even though
his mouth was full of
pooris, he said, 'Ōm . . .'

Grandpa Rides in a Rocket

They knew the fair was coming to town, because one morning, bright posters were plastered all over the place on walls, in shops. They hung from hooks alongside the legs of lamb in the butcher's and the bunches of bananas in the greengrocers, or they were pinned on to notice boards in public buildings, in the library, in the town hall.

GRAND BANK HOLIDAY FAIR, the posters proclaimed. FUN FOR ALL THE FAMILY; AMUSEMENTS, STALLS, PONY RIDES, THRILLS AND SPILLS AND SPECIAL ATTRACTIONS.

'We must go to that,' said Dad. 'Keep a look out.'

Well, they didn't really need to keep a look out. You couldn't miss it. One day, all the roads through the town were clogged with battered cars and vans, trailers and caravans, lorries and trucks. Clowns with silly faces mingled with the shoppers and thrust leaflets into their hands; a girl walked by on stilts, ten feet high, waving and smiling.

'I'd like to do that,' sighed Neetu.

When they went home and told Grandpa Chatterji about the fair, his eyes gleamed with pleasure. 'I love fairs,' he beamed. 'I love watching all the elephants and camels and horses and bullock carts, and all the women in their glittering skirts and saris, and all the men wearing their most colourful turbans. Oh good, oh good!' And he rubbed his hands together in anticipation.

'But, Grandpa,' exclaimed Sanjay in a puzzled voice, 'fairs here aren't like that.'

'You're thinking of an Indian fair,' laughed Mum. 'This will be quite different.'

'Oh!' said Grandpa, looking rather downcast. 'What will this fair be like?'

'It will have Dodgem Cars and merry-go-rounds and waltzers and a ghost train. It

will have lots of stalls with games and competitions. I won a fluffy cat last year. I guessed the right number when I tossed in a coin,' Neetu told him.

'Grandpa, will you go on the rockets with me?' begged Sanjay. 'Everyone else is too scared.'

'I'll go on anything,' boasted Grandpa, looking excited again.

'You'll remember your age, Pa, that's what you'll do,' said Mum firmly.

But Grandpa Chatterji couldn't

remember his age. He was ageless.
Sometimes he seemed as old and as wise as
the universe, and other times, it was as
though he had only just been born and had
come into the world full of wonder. Now, he
looked forward to the fair with all the
excitement of a child. He rushed about
saying, 'Come on, then. Let's go, let's go!
What are we waiting for?'

'We'll go when it's dark, Grandpa. It's
much more fun,' they told him.

As soon as it was dark, the nearby
playing fields were ablaze with light and loud

music pulsated through the air. It was magic. No one could resist it. Everyone filled their pockets with money, and soon, all the roads leading to the fair were thronging with families. Mum, Dad, Grandpa, Neetu and Sanjay joined the crowds. Grandpa kept hopping up and down, his eyes wide as saucers. 'Look! Look!' He pointed at glittering machines which lit up the sky as bright as a city. He looked at the giant Rocket Ride, which rose up into the night like a space station, its rockets orbiting and spinning like shooting stars. 'Let's see it all!'

cried Grandpa Chatterji.

He was like a moth attracted by the fiery brightness. Not only were there garlands of fairy lights looped from stall to stall all bobbing about in the evening breeze, but there were the more powerful patterns of light from the different machines, which flashed on and off in rhythm to the thundering music. The music was so loud, they could hardly hear themselves speak.

But this wasn't a place for speaking. This was a place for looking and listening and doing. Everyone communicated in sign language. Children held out empty palms to be filled with coins; they pointed at ice creams, hot dogs or candy floss, and the only human sounds which could

be heard, were the high-pitched
screams coming from the Ghost Train
or the Rocket Ride, as people were
whirled round and round, higher and
higher, faster and faster.

Grandpa kept rushing over to the
different attractions shouting, 'I want
to try this! I want to try that!' And he
disappeared from sight for minutes on
end. They would find him at the Rifle
Range, or trying to hook a wrist watch
with a fishing line; or tossing darts at
playing cards in the hope of winning a
huge, pink teddy bear.

The longest time he was out of
sight, was when he went into the
fortune-teller's tent to have his palm
read. Mum and Dad looked

everywhere, trying at the same time to keep
track of Neetu and Sanjay.

'Can't you keep your father in order?'
Dad said to Mum in exasperation.

Then just when they thought they had
lost him for good, he emerged from the tent
with a smug grin on his face. 'I went in to
have my fortune told,' he shouted, 'but it was
I who told the fortune-teller's fortune. She's a
fraud. She didn't know anything. All she
could say was, you have been on a long
journey. Then I took her hand, and told her
that she had just moved house; her husband
had a new job and her daughter had just

given birth to twins. She was astounded.'

'Was it true?' asked Neetu.

'Of course it was true,' retorted Grandpa. 'I know what I'm doing.'

'I want to go on the Rocket Ride,' shouted Sanjay.

'No!' said Mum and Dad together. 'You can't go alone, and none of us will go with you.'

'Grandpa would,' said Sanjay, looking slyly up at Grandpa.

Grandpa Chatterji opened his mouth . . . but Dad whisked Sanjay away. 'Look! We're right near the Dodgem Cars. You like those.'

'Oh, yes! Let's go on the Dodgem Cars!' cried Sanjay. He showed Grandpa the little red, yellow and blue cars which raced round dodging and bumping into each other.

'I can't drive!' cried Grandpa.

'Neither can I!' laughed Sanjay, 'but it doesn't matter. All you do is press a pedal and steer.'

'Come on then! Let's go!' cried Grandpa eagerly. 'I've always wanted to drive a car!'

They all went on the Dodgem Cars, even Mum and Dad. Everyone had two goes, except Grandpa, who had three. He would have stayed on them all night. He was like a demon driver, hurtling around, crashing and

bumping, twisting and turning. But in the
end, Neetu dragged him off so that he would
go with her on the Waltzer.

Grandpa looked back wistfully at the
Dodgem Cars. 'Do you think it's too late for
me to learn to drive?' he asked.

'Much too late,' said Dad firmly.

On the way to the Waltzer, they passed
the Rocket Ride. 'Please come on the Rocket
with me, Grandpa!' begged Sanjay.

'No, Sanjay!' protested Neetu.

'Grandpa's coming with me on the Waltzer.'

Grandpa stopped for a moment and looked at the great steely arms of the machine, and the shining silver rockets fixed to the ends. They soared up into the sky, spun around and then dipped down at great speed. It looked so exciting.

'Take me! Take me!' begged Sanjay.

'Looks exciting,' murmured Grandpa. 'I'd like a go on that.'

'Oh no you won't,' Mum yelled as sternly as she could above the din. 'You're too old and Sanjay's too young.'

'Hmm!' snorted Grandpa, and carried on with Neetu to the Waltzer.

So they whirled about on the Waltzer. Then they went on to the Helter-Skelter, sliding down on cushions and landing in a tumble at the bottom. They stumbled round the Funnyhouse laughing at themselves in the distorted mirrors, and they frightened themselves silly in the Ghost Train, screaming until their throats were sore.

When Mum said finally, 'It's time to go home,' everyone groaned – especially Grandpa.

'Must we?' he wailed.

'Really, Pa, you're as bad as the children!' grumbled his daughter.

'I know, I know!' Grandpa hung his head like an old crow, though his eyes never stopped glittering. 'But there's no harm. It's good to be young, even when you're old.'

On their way out, they passed the great Rocket Ride. Grandpa stopped again, and looked at the gleaming rockets, whirling through the night sky. He couldn't resist. 'I cannot leave Great Britain without going on a Rocket Ride!' he exclaimed seriously. 'I want to go on the Rocket.'

'Me too, Grandpa!' shrieked Sanjay. 'Me too. Mum, you said I could if I found an adult willing to take me, and Grandpa's an adult, isn't he?'

'I wonder, sometimes,' muttered Dad.

'What did you say?' asked Sanjay.

'I said . . .' Dad faltered . . . 'Yes, he's an adult, I suppose.'

'That's settled then. We will go on the Rocket, my boy!' Grandpa Chatterji beamed. Suddenly, Grandpa had decided to act as head of the family. No one could really say no to him once he had made up his mind, not even Mum and Dad. 'Don't worry,

daughter,' he reassured Sanjay's mother.
'We'll be fine. We'll hang on to each other for
safety, won't we!'

Sanjay laughed triumphantly, and
holding Grandpa's hand, they excitedly
joined the queue for the next Rocket Ride.

'Neetu, Mum and I
will go on the Beetle-Bug
Ride while you two make
yourselves sick,' said Dad,
shrugging with defeat.
'Let's meet here
afterwards.'

They all agreed and then separated.

Sanjay looked at the shining bodies of the
rockets. They didn't look scary at all from
the ground.

'I don't see what's so frightening about

those rockets,' cried Grandpa. 'What's all the fuss about?'

'I don't know,' answered Sanjay innocently, although he knew that even his best friend, who was such a toughie, had been scared out of his wits when he went on it last year, and had said he would never go again.

They studied people's faces as the Rocket came to a standstill and the people clambered out. It's true, not many were smiling. Some looked quite green and grim. But no one would admit it had been horrible. Grandpa and Sanjay heard voices saying, 'Phew, that was terrific, wasn't it?' And others replying, 'Yeah! It was really great!'

Grandpa and Sanjay chose a rocket for themselves. They climbed inside and strapped the seat belts on. A man came round collecting the money, and then when all the rockets had filled up, slowly, slowly, the machine began to move.

At first it started gently. They could look out and see all the people down below.

'Look! There's Neetu and Mum and Dad queuing for the Beetle-Bug Ride.' Sanjay waved frantically, but within a second they were gone, as the Rocket turned, and next time round, they were already too high to make out anybody.

They were only in the Rocket for three minutes, but it was three minutes of hell. Within twenty seconds, they were rotating at a great height,

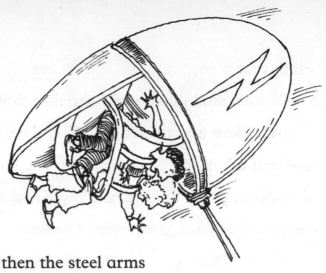

and then the steel arms

dipped them down at great speed, so that

they were sure they would be tossed into

eternity, before it whisked them up again. By

the time one minute was up, Sanjay had his

face buried in Grandpa's shoulder,

whimpering with terror as they were spun

about and tipped and somersaulted.

Grandpa shut his eyes. It would have

been possible to think that nothing had

upset him, except that the knuckles of his

fingers were white, as he gripped the arms

of his seat.

'Get me off, get me off!' shrieked Sanjay.

But there was no getting off. At last, after
two and a half minutes, the Rocket began to
slow down bit by bit and gradually drop
lower and lower.

When it
finally came to a standstill,
Grandpa and Sanjay were frozen with shock
and didn't get out.

'Having another go, are you?' asked the
man, holding out his hand for more money.

'Oh no! No!' gulped Grandpa. 'We're going, we're going!'

The whole world was still tipping and turning, as they got out of the Rocket and wobbled their way to the exit. They waited, silent with dizziness, until at last Mum, Dad and Neetu came bounding over. They had had a wonderful ride on the Beetle-Bug.

'Oh, Grandpa! You must go on it!' cried Neetu. 'Come with me now, I'd love another go.'

'No, no!' groaned Grandpa. 'I couldn't manage another ride.'

'Are you two all right?' asked Mum peering at them closely. 'Was it good?'

'It was great!' said Sanjay in a dull voice. He felt sick.

'I've never had such an experience,' said

Grandpa, swaying slightly.

'Hmm,' said Dad with a knowing look. 'You both look a bit green. I think it's time we went home.'

Mum popped Sanjay and Neetu into the bath and quickly got them ready for bed. Then she said, 'Just go and say "good night" to Grandpa.' They went downstairs, but Grandpa wasn't watching television with Dad, so they said good night to Dad, and went back up. They went to Grandpa's room and knocked on the door.

'Come in,' said a soft voice.

When they opened the door, there was Grandpa upside down, standing on his head on the rug.

'Oh, Pa! Haven't you had enough of

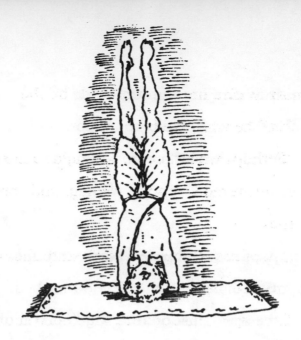

being upside down for one night!' laughed
Mum.

'I stand upside down so that I can feel the
right way up,' smiled Grandpa.

'Good night, Grandpa Chatterji,' said
Neetu, bending down on her knees so that
she could give her grandfather a kiss.

'Good night, Grandpa Chatterji,' said
Sanjay, pressing his mouth close to his
grandfather's ear. 'Shall we go back

tomorrow and have another ride on the Rocket?' he whispered.

'Perhaps when I come to England next time,' answered Grandpa weakly, and shut his eyes.

'Good night, then,' they all said again as they reached the door.

Grandpa Chatterji wriggled his feet in the air.

When Grandpa
Leicester came to
stay

Mum was scurrying about. Dad was fiddling

with his tie. He always fiddled with his tie

when he was nervous. Neetu and Sanjay

looked a little solemn. Today Neetu was

wearing a dress and Sanjay was wearing grey trousers and a jacket.

Grandpa Chatterji was still only wearing his *dhoti*. He had done his yoga exercises, he had bathed, he had cleaned his teeth, he had washed out his mouth and nose and throat by gargling and snorting with salt water, and he had said his prayers.

When he came down to breakfast, his face was shining with cleanliness and good humour, and he was surprised to notice that everyone looked a little glum.

'What is happening?' he asked. 'Why the long faces?'

He looked at his grandchildren. 'Is something wrong?'

'Didn't you know?' cried Neetu. 'Grandpa Leicester is visiting us today! You'd better get dressed.'

'I am dressed,' corrected Grandpa Chatterji.

'Grandpa Leicester will call you "jungly" if you don't put on a suit,' said Neetu doubtfully.

'Don't worry, Grandpa Leicester won't find anything wrong with me when we meet,' replied Grandpa Chatterji, reassuringly.

'I must start preparing food,' murmured Mother. 'Grandpa Leicester is rather fussy about what he eats.' Anxiously, she hurried away.

Soon a smell of cooking drifted through

the house. Sanjay screwed up his nose. 'Oh, no! We'll have to eat Grandpa Leicester's favourite food.'

'I'll go and help your mother with the cooking,' said Grandpa Chatterji. 'Maybe I can produce something that you will like, and Grandpa Leicester will like too.'

'Is there room for me in the kitchen?' he asked his daughter.

'There isn't very much space,' she answered warily. 'How many gas rings do you need?'

'One will do!' replied Grandpa Chatterji. He put on a large apron which looped round his neck and covered him from his neck down to his knees. Then he got out a chopping board, and a mixing bowl and a packet of *gram* flour. He found three large onions,

garlic, potatoes, cauliflower, carrots,
tomatoes, pepper, salt and two or three
packets of yellow, brown and orange powder.

Bit by bit, Grandpa spread and spread.
Soon he had taken over the whole kitchen.
The table and every bit of worktop was
covered with something, and each time Mum
moved in one direction, Grandpa shifted her
to another. She was in despair.

'Too many cooks spoil the broth, Father!'
she told him. 'Why don't you leave me to get
on with it now?'

But Grandpa Chatterji said, 'Don't take
any notice of me. I won't get in your way,'
and he carried on with his preparations.

But Grandpa did get in her way, and
stubbornly refused to go. Finally, Mum
clutched her head. 'There's no room for me

to mix my spices. There's no room for me to prepare my spinach and ladies fingers. In fact there's no room for me at all! Either you go or I must go!' she declared. 'There's no room for both of us!'

'Why don't you leave it to me. Relax, have a bath, and put on your best sari,' suggested Grandpa Chatterji soothingly. 'Leave the food to me!'

Mum shrugged with defeat and fled. 'Don't blame me if the meal is ruined and Grandpa Leicester never comes here again!' she wailed to her husband.

Neetu and Sanjay peeped into the kitchen.

'Grandpa's doing the cooking!' exclaimed Neetu.

'I don't think I'm going to like what

Grandpa cooks,' whispered Sanjay, looking suspiciously at the different ingredients. 'I only really like pizza and chips.'

'You liked my *pooris*,' reminded Grandpa, whose sharp ears had picked up Sanjay's words.

'You didn't put hot peppery stuff in your *pooris*,' answered Sanjay.

'I promise I'm not going to make this hot either,' smiled Grandpa, 'but it will be tasty, so tasty, that you'll gobble them all up. Now then, I need a hand. All these vegetables need washing and chopping up. I want the potatoes and carrots diced into small chunks; I want the cauliflower broken into little flowers and someone is going to have to slice the onions.

'I'll do it!' shouted Neetu eagerly.

'I'll do it!' yelled Sanjay.

The kitchen came alive with smells. Smoke and steam poured out through the doors and windows. Grandpa chopped and sliced and tossed and fried and rolled. A big saucepan of fat smoked to boiling point on the gas ring. A large mixing bowl full of batter stood nearby all lumpy with chopped up vegetables. Grandpa was just about to ladle out a portion of batter and drop it, sizzling into the fat, when the doorbell rang.

'Oh, no!' exclaimed the children, 'Grandpa Leicester has arrived already!'

They peeped into the hall and saw Dad opening the front door. 'Father! It's you!' came his voice. 'You're early. We weren't expecting you so soon.'

They saw Grandpa Leicester standing

there so smart and stern. He wore a dark grey pinstriped suit; he wore a pure white French shirt with a stiff collar and cuffs which showed exactly two inches beneath the sleeve of his jacket; he had on his smart Rotary Club tie, and on his feet were shiny, mirror-bright black Italian leather shoes.

'Look!' hissed Sanjay. 'Grandpa Leicester's come in his new Jaguar. Do you think he'll take us for a ride?' He stared longingly beyond his grandfather to the beautiful, sleek, low, dark-green saloon car which crouched in the road.

'Shouldn't think so,' muttered Neetu. 'Not after you went and got chocolate all over the seats of his last car.'

They heard Mum coming downstairs, swishing and tinkling. She had put on one of her best saris and wore her bangles and earrings. Grandpa Leicester remarked admiringly, 'Oh, don't you look lovely, my dear!'

'Welcome, *Papaji*!' Mother murmured. 'I do hope you had an uneventful journey.'

'Well! Where is everybody? Where is Chatterji *sahib*?' Grandpa Leicester demanded, stepping inside. 'And where are my grandchildren?'

Neetu stared in horror at Sanjay and pulled him back inside the kitchen. 'Look at you!' she gasped.

Sanjay stared at Neetu. 'Look at you!'

Then they both looked at Grandpa
Chatterji. 'Look at Grandpa!' Grandpa
Chatterji had yellow batter plastered all up
his arms to his elbows, Sanjay looked like a
clown, with his hair covered in flour, and
blobs of batter on his nose and cheeks; and as
for Neetu, she had red eyes running with
tears from slicing onions, and her best dress
was streaked with masala powders.

'We can't go out and meet Grandpa Leicester like this!' they cried.

'They'll be here in a minute.' They could hear Mum answering Grandpa Leicester, in a flustery voice. 'Come into the living room and relax. Let me bring you a cup of . . .'

'Aaaachoo!' Sanjay sneezed. He had got flour up his nose.

Grandpa Leicester immediately strode to the kitchen and flung open the door. 'So, my little ones! You are hiding in here, are you?' he cried jovially, then stopped with astonishment. There before him stood Grandpa Chatterji, Neetu and Sanjay all covered in batter and flour looking like white ghosts, and wishing that, like spirits, they could disappear.

If there was one thing Grandpa Leicester

couldn't bear, it was mess. They could tell by the critical way his eyes swept around, that he could see nothing but mess; messy children, messy kitchen and a messy Grandpa Chatterji. With sinking hearts, they waited to hear his severe voice telling them off. 'I don't like my grandchildren to look messy.'

Mum looked as if she wished she could disappear through the floor. 'Sanjay! Look at your best jacket and trousers! Neetu! Look at the state of your beautiful dress! Oh, Pa! How could you let these children get into such a mess?' she accused Grandpa Chatterji.

'We've been cooking,' exclaimed Grandpa Chatterji, undaunted. Then he strode up to Grandpa Leicester with a broad,

beaming face and clasped him in his arms.
'How good to see you again!'

'Hey, hey!' cried Grandpa Leicester,
aghast, and pulled himself away from
Grandpa Chatterji's floury embrace. 'Oh, no!
Look at my best suit!'

Everyone stared
in horror at the
white imprints of
hands on each of
Grandpa Leicester's
dark, pinstriped
shoulders.

Mum grabbed
Neetu and Sanjay
and fled upstairs.

'Ma,' whispered
Neetu fearfully.

'What will Grandpa Leicester do to Grandpa Chatterji?'

'I don't know,' she answered in a shaky voice. 'Perhaps he'll just go home again.'

Alone together in the kitchen, the two grandfathers faced each other. Grandpa Leicester opened his mouth to growl a protest at the state of his suit, but no words came out. Grandpa Chatterji tipped his head on one side and smiled like an angel. Then he grabbed Grandpa Leicester by the arm, putting more floury imprints on his sleeves, and pulled him over to the cooker, murmuring sweetly, 'Don't worry about your suit! It will all brush off. Because you are the honoured guest, you must be the first to taste one of my very best *pakoras*. I have made them specially for you.'

Grandpa Chatterji ladled up some batter and dropped it into the smoking oil. There was a sizzling and a splattering and a squealing, as the batter made a golden brown crispy shell all around the vegetables. Grandpa Chatterji dropped in another and another, and soon the pan was bobbing with *pakoras*. As each one was done, he scooped it out with a spatula and dropped it on to a plate covered with a paper towel.

'Eat, eat!' he urged, thrusting the plate under Grandpa Leicester's nose. 'Tell me if you have ever tasted a better *pakora*!'

'Ow!' yelled Grandpa Leicester, as some fat spat on his skin. 'Leave me alone! I'm not hungry yet. I'd rather wait for the proper meal.'

'Oh, but I just want you to test it for me.

Tell me if it needs more salt or more *masalas*!' insisted Grandpa Chatterji.

If it had been anyone else in the world, Grandpa Leicester would already have marched out of the kitchen, exploding with anger at the state of his best suit. But somehow, Grandpa Chatterji looked him in the eye with his round, dark, deep-as-oceans eyes, and held the plate so close to his  nose that the smell of the *pakora* went straight up his nostrils and made his mouth water.

Grandpa Leicester couldn't resist. 'Oh, all right,' he grunted reluctantly, and popped the *pakora* into his mouth.

'Ah, ah, ah!' he hopped up and down with his mouth open. The *pakora* was piping hot. He flapped his hand in front of his mouth, gradually chewing off little bits and swallowing them. They were delicious. With difficulty, he continued to frown, as if he were still furious about his suit, but the taste of Grandpa Chatterji's *pakoras* was so delicious that, instead of shouting with anger, he ate up all the *pakoras* and held out the plate for more. Gradually his frowns gave way to blissful smiles.

'They're delicious. The best I've ever had. How did you do it? Show me!' He bent over the bowl of batter and watched carefully how

Grandpa Chatterji ladled the batter into the oil.

'We need some more vegetables!' cried Grandpa Chatterji. 'Children?' He looked around for Neetu and Sanjay. 'Oh, dear, my assistants have gone. Here!' he thrust a knife into Grandpa Leicester's hand. 'Chop up some more onions, spinach, potatoes and carrots for me while I boil some eggs.'

Time passed. The two grandfathers were still in the kitchen behind closed doors. Neetu and Sanjay had cleaned themselves up and changed their clothes; Dad sat uneasily in the living room, while Mum paced up and down, imagining that lunch would be a total disaster.

'When are we going to eat?' moaned Neetu.

'I'm starving!' groaned Sanjay.

Suddenly, the two grandfathers appeared in the doorway. Grandpa Chatterji was still in his *dhoti* with an overall on top, and Grandpa Leicester – everyone looked in amazement at Grandpa Leicester. He had taken off his pinstriped jacket, removed his smart Rotarian tie and rolled up the sleeves of his sparkling white French shirt. Most incredible of all, he had tied a frilly pinny round his waist.

'Lunch is served!' they both exclaimed, beaming with delight.

What a feast the two grandfathers had prepared. The table was overflowing with food. There were bowls of *pakoras*, plates of *pooris*, tureens of turmeric-coloured lentils and dark green spinach. There were

casseroles of vegetables
and egg curries, saucers of
pickles, dishes of yogurt
and chopped cucumber,
and platters piled high with
snow-white rice.

'Eat, eat!' begged the
grandfathers, passing
round the plates.

Everybody ate.
Nobody really spoke,
except to exclaim,
'Delicious! Wonderful! Can
I have another *pakora*? You
two should open a
restaurant!'

Grandpa Chatterji was
right. Even though there

was no pizza and chips, everybody found

something they liked eating – even Sanjay.

They seemed to eat all afternoon till

there was barely a dish which hadn't been

scraped clean. Then Mum, Dad and the

children said they would do the washing up.

Grandpa Leicester stuck his thumbs in the waist of his trousers and said, 'I've eaten too much and my trousers are too tight.' Then he looked enviously at Grandpa Chatterji. 'I do like your *dhoti*. It's years since I wore one.'

'I have a spare one in my room,' beamed Grandpa Chatterji. 'Please come up and put it on.'

When the children had finished helping in the kitchen they went looking for their grandpas. The house was strangely quiet. Where were they? Perhaps they were snoozing in front of the television; but there was no one in the living room. Perhaps they were sitting in the garden; but there was no one in the garden.

They went upstairs. Grandpa Chatterji's bedroom door was a little ajar. Neetu and Sanjay quietly peered inside. Then they looked at each other and hunched their shoulders in secret laughter. Grandpa Leicester had taken off his uncomfortable pinstriped suit, his French shirt and his Rotarian tie. He had taken off his stiff, shining black leather Italian shoes. His chest was bare and his legs and feet were bare. All he wore was a thin cotton *dhoti*, and he sat cross-legged next to Grandpa Chatterji on his special Indian carpet. Their eyes were shut and their faces were serene and they breathed in for a very long time . . . and out for a very long time.

'What are you doing, Grandpa?' whispered Neetu.

'We're digesting,' said Grandpa Leicester.

'And meditating,' said Grandpa
Chatterji.

'When you've finished digesting and
meditating, will you take us for a ride in your
new Jaguar?' whispered Sanjay tentatively.

'Jaguar?' asked Grandpa Chatterji
opening one eye. 'I've heard of riding *on* an
elephant or being pulled *by* a horse, but I've
never heard of riding *in* a jaguar.'

'You've never heard of riding in a Jaguar?' asked Grandpa Leicester, opening one eye. Then he opened his other eye. 'Shall we take Grandpa Chatterji for a ride in a Jaguar?' he asked his grandchildren with a wink.

'Yes, yes!' shouted the children.

'Have you got any chocolate in your pocket?' asked Grandpa Leicester, sternly.

'No, no!' shouted the children. 'Come on, Grandpa!' and the children grabbed Grandpa Chatterji and Grandpa Leicester and heaved them to their feet.

'There were lots of things I thought I would do when I came to England, but I never thought I would ride in a jaguar!' exclaimed Grandpa Chatterji, somewhat puzzled.

They all went downstairs. They opened
the door. There was the Jaguar waiting for
them, all glossy and shining.

'Ah!' Grandpa Chatterji gave a heartfelt sigh at the beauty of the machine. 'So that is what you call a jaguar! Yes, let's carry on with our digesting in a Jaguar.'

'I think I'd better put on my shoes,' said Grandpa Leicester. 'I can't drive barefoot.' So he put on his black, shiny, Italian shoes. They looked a little odd with a *dhoti*, but nobody cared. They sank into the soft leathery seats. Grandpa Leicester turned the key. The car roared into life with throbbing power. Then they sped down the road, silent and swift as a jungle cat.

'This is a chariot worthy of the gods!' exclaimed Grandpa Chatterji, overcome with delight. 'It's as good as flying!'

'Ahhah!' agreed Grandpa Leicester, bobbing his head with pleasure. Then he leaned forward to the polished walnut dashboard and opened a compartment. He took out a tin of sweets and passed it to the children in the back of the car. 'You may have one each of these,' he said, 'so long as they stay in your mouth and you don't get any sticky stuff on my beautiful seats.'

'Oh, thank you, Grandpa Leicester!' cried Neetu, gratefully.

She and Sanjay each popped a sweet into their mouths.

'You know,' Sanjay whispered in Neetu's ear. 'I think I like Grandpa Leicester after all.'

Neetu sucked her sweet and nodded. She caught Grandpa Chatterji looking at her through the rear mirror. He winked. 'I like both our grandpas,' she said, winking back.

The Poppy Field

Into the sunshine they stepped. It was a
miracle. The air was like silk, sliding softly
over their skin. There was a smell of grass
and flowers and of earth drying out in
steamy vapours rising up and up. The
puddles which had glistened in the gutters
like dark mirrors, now reflected blue sky;
the streets and pavements looked clean

and washed.

Grandpa Chatterji shook his head with wonder. Why, only yesterday, he had been so cold, that he had put on his long johns, shirt, three woolly jumpers and two pairs of socks; he had wound a thick woollen scarf round his neck and put a woolly hat on his head which he pulled down right over his ears; and still

he had felt cold. That morning, he had tried to say his prayers out in the garden under the tree, standing on one leg to welcome a new day. But it was so much harder when he was shivery and cold and all bundled up like that.

Finally, he had made a hot water bottle and, clutching it tightly to his chest had muttered, 'I'm going back to bed.' Neetu and Sanjay had peeped into his room an hour later. Grandpa had been lying in his bedroll with the blanket pulled up to his chin. Two deep brown eyes had stared miserably at them over the top.

'England is too cold for me!' he had groaned. 'How long will this last?'

The children shook their heads. Who could tell?

Now a sliver of gold burst through the cracks in the curtain, and when they looked outside, there was the sun riding high through the sky and it was as though the world had been created all over again.

'That's more like it!' exclaimed Grundpa, stretching out his limbs to absorb the warmth. But he was still disbelieving. Could the weather change so quickly from cold to hot? So he still put on his long johns, shirt, three woolly jumpers and two pairs of socks; and he still wrapped a scarf round his neck and pulled a woolly cap down over his ears.

'Grandpa? Won't you be too hot?' asked Neetu, looking at his red face.

'Well, perhaps I can take off one of my woolly jumpers,' agreed Grandpa. So he took off one. 'That's better!' he said.

Sanjay saw a trickle of perspiration sliding down Grandpa's cheek from beneath his woolly cap. 'Grandpa, aren't you baking under that hat and scarf?'

Grandpa thought about it. He went outside and put out a hand to test the temperature. Yes, it was a much warmer day. So he removed his hat and scarf. 'That's better,' he said.

Mum came in. She was wearing light cotton trousers and a short-sleeved blouse. Grandpa looked at her doubtfully. 'Aren't you too cold like that? This isn't India.'

'No, Father, this isn't India. This is England, where the weather can change

from hot to cold all in one day. You have to
be prepared. Yesterday was cold, but today is
really warm, much too warm for
you to be wearing two
pullovers and two pairs of
socks and your long johns!'

Grandpa nodded
ruefully, and took off another
pullover and one pair of socks.
'That's better,' he sighed. 'Now I feel
comfortable. Now I feel like a walk.'

He jumped up, suddenly full of energy.
'Come on everybody! Let's go walking! I
want to find the poppy field!'

'What poppy field?' asked Neetu and
Sanjay.

'What poppy field?' asked Mum and
Dad.

No one knew of any poppy field.

'Let's go, let's go,' urged Grandpa. 'I can't come all this way to England and not see a poppy field. I know there's a poppy field. Trust me! We'll find one.'

'But, Father,' Mum cried in a mystified voice. 'It's too early for poppies. They come in the summer and it's only April and, in any case, you won't find poppy fields in a town!'

'Come along, come along!' insisted Grandpa. 'I'll show you!'

Mum, Neetu and Sanjay looked at each other and grinned.

'Oh, well! It is Saturday, and there's nothing planned. It's such a nice day, so it won't hurt to go hunting for a poppy field that doesn't exist; and a walk does you good,' agreed Mum. So they followed

Grandpa outside.

'Are you coming, dear?' Mum asked Dad before she closed the front door.

'I'm not going on any wild goose chase,' snorted Dad. 'Anyway, I want to watch the cricket on telly.'

'See you later then!' she cried.

'I hope so!' laughed Dad. 'If your father doesn't walk you all the way to Timbuktu.'

Grandpa Chatterji strode out ahead with his umbrella in his hand. 'Just in case it rains,' he had muttered. 'As you never seem to know where you are in this country!' He stuck the spike out in front of him to point the way.

Mum, Neetu and

Sanjay followed behind. Where would
Grandpa lead them? They walked down to
the end of the road and reached a T-junction.
Grandpa stopped and held up his umbrella
as if it would somehow tell him which way to
go, then he turned smartly right.

'Are we nearly there?' asked Sanjay,
beginning to dawdle.

'Just a little further,' replied Grandpa,
cheerily.

They walked and walked and walked,
passing row upon row of houses. People were
working in their gardens or washing the car.

Some stopped and waved; and some cried out, 'Where are you going on this nice, fine day?'

'We're going to find a poppy field for Grandpa!' shouted Neetu.

Then the people had shaken their heads in puzzlement. 'This is the town not the country. You won't find a poppy field round here – and anyway, it's the wrong time of year.'

'Never mind,' Mum reassured them. 'It will give us a good walk in the sunshine.'

They came to a small road which they had never walked down before. There was an old grey stone church. It stood in the middle of a triangular churchyard on the corner of a fork in the road. A sleek, black cat crouched in the long, overgrown grass among the tombstones. Grandpa stopped and held up his umbrella. The point swung in one direction, then in another and then back again. The cat watched; the children watched and Mum watched.

'Are we nearly there?' asked Sanjay.

'It can't be far now,' murmured Grandpa

encouragingly.

'Which way do we go, Grandpa?' cried Neetu.

'This way, this way!' exclaimed Grandpa confidently, and marched off down the left fork. As if curious to know where they were going, the black cat followed.

They walked and walked and walked.

Then the road suddenly ended. There they were standing in a quiet cul-de-sac, where a semi-circle of little brick houses seemed to be spying on them secretly through their net-curtained windows. The neat gardens formed a lush semi-circle of lawns, bushes, flower beds and trees. The gardens were divided one from the other by a mixture of walls, hedges and fences. They couldn't see any road which would take them further.

'When are we getting there?' moaned Sanjay. It seemed to him that they had walked quite far enough.

'Not long, not long!' cried Grandpa. He lifted

up his umbrella. He seemed to be relying on it to lead the way. It turned a vague circle in the air above his head and looked inclined to take them back the way they had come. Grandpa shut his eyes and stood on one leg.

'Are you praying, Grandpa?' asked Neetu.

Grandpa opened one serious eye and stared down at her. 'I'm thinking,' he answered.

'I'll think with you,' said Neetu, and stood on one leg with her eyes closed.

'Perhaps we should give up now, and go home,' suggested Mum.

'Don't be faint-hearted, my dear! You should know that you can trust your father. Be patient,' he ordered, and closed his eyes again.

So Mum sat on a low wall and admired the pretty gardens while the black cat coiled itself round their legs purring loudly.

Suddenly, the cat darted across the road and sprang on to a wall. It stretched forward on to its front paws, spreading out its claws, then backwards. Neetu opened her eyes. She stopped standing on one leg and watched the cat, smiling. It leapt down and disappeared between two gardens.

'That's funny!' thought Neetu. 'Where did it go?' She ran across the road to where the cat had been sitting. Then she saw

that it had walked up a narrow
little lane, almost hidden between
the wall and an overgrown
hedge.

'Hey! Look what I've found!'
Neetu cried. 'There's a path
here.'

Grandpa's umbrella swung in
Neetu's direction. 'Good!' he
exclaimed. 'That must be the
way we have to go.'

It was a narrow, leafy lane,
overhung with the branches of
trees and trailing ivy. It led them
all the way between people's
houses and back gardens, until
suddenly it came to some steps
leading up to a wooden bridge.

'Good heavens!' cried Mum. 'It's brought us to an old railway line.'

Neetu and Sanjay raced up on to the bridge. They peered down through the iron bars. 'This can't be a railway line! There aren't any rails!' cried Neetu.

'Won't we see a train, then?' moaned Sanjay with disappointment. He thought that seeing a train would be much more exciting than finding a poppy field.

'I'm afraid it's a disused track now,' said his mother. 'They've turned it into a path for walkers and cyclists.'

'Then that is where we must go,' said Grandpa firmly, and strode across the bridge and down the other side.

The black cat was waiting. It slid through the long grass which wavered across the path. It seemed to know they would come.

'We've lived here for years,' exclaimed Mum, 'and I never knew about this track. I wonder where it goes?'

'To the poppy field, of course!' answered Grandpa, and set off at a rapid pace. The others had to run to keep up.

The railway banks rose steeply on either side, bursting with flowers – all white and

yellow and pink and blue. There were parson's lace and ragwort and celandine and campion and clusters of violets and straggles of forget-me-nots, all nodding gently as if talking to each other.

'Which ones are poppies?' asked Grandpa.

'None of these,' stated Mum firmly. 'I told you. Poppies come later.'

'Humm!' snorted Grandpa, disbelievingly, and continued striding ahead.

'I wish I'd brought my bike,' sighed Sanjay.

'We'll come back here again! It's a wonderful place for you to ride bicycles. So safe, without any traffic to worry about,' Mum promised him.

'But I want to see Grandpa's poppy

field,' cried Neetu impatiently. 'You do know there is one, don't you, Grandpa? You aren't wrong, are you?'

'Of course I'm not wrong. I'll find a poppy field. Just you see!' Grandpa wagged his finger at them confidently. 'Trust me.'

They saw a round black hole looming ahead. It was like a huge black eye. 'What's

that?' gasped Sanjay.

'It's a railway tunnel,' Mum told him.

It looked exciting. Sanjay and Neetu began running towards it. The black cat overtook them and darted ahead.

For a moment, they paused on the edge between bright sunlight, and the black darkness of the tunnel. They could feel the sudden chill on their skin, and their voices echoed strangely. They hesitated and looked back. Mum and Grandpa were hurrying towards them. They smiled reassuringly, so Neetu and Sanjay ran on inside the tunnel. The black cat stayed back in the sunlight, its fur suddenly standing on end, and its tail stiffening. Then it sprang up the bank into the long grass and disappeared over the top.

Far, far ahead, at the end of the

darkness, the children could now see something round and silver gleaming in the distance. 'What's that?' whispered Sanjay. His words echoed round their heads.

Mum's voice answered back softly. 'It's the light at the end of the tunnel!' she chuckled.

Somehow, Sanjay and Neetu no longer wanted to run on ahead. They waited for Grandpa and Mum and, fixing their eyes on

the silvery light, they walked together, steadily towards the other end.

Nearer and nearer they went. Nobody spoke, but there was a feeling of magic in the air. They were about to make a discovery. They were almost at the end of the tunnel, when suddenly, just as they were about to step out into daylight, Grandpa stopped dead in his tracks.

'What is it, Father?' asked Mum with alarm.

'It's the poppy field. It's out there. I told you we'd find it,' he breathed.

He closed his eyes and pressed his hands together in front of him with his elbows sticking outwards and did not take another step forwards.

Bursting with excitement, Neetu ran out

of the tunnel. She stood, blinded for a few moments by the bright daylight. She looked eagerly around. 'Where are the poppies, Grandpa?' cried Neetu. She ran further up the track looking this way and that. 'I can't see any poppies,' she wailed, her voice rising with disappointment. She ran back to the tunnel. Grandpa was still standing inside.

'Grandpa, you were wrong. There are no poppies here,' she cried accusingly.

'Ssh!' whispered Mum, comfortingly. 'I think Grandpa has his own special eye. He's seeing the poppies in his own mind with his inner eye. If you shut your eyes, perhaps you

will see a field of poppies, too.'

Neetu and Sanjay gazed around them.
The sloping banks on either side of the
railway track were entirely green, with long
stems of waving grass, and the black cat
stalking across the top. They closed their eyes
and, inside their heads, tried to imagine the
banks all red with poppies.

Grandpa never came out of the tunnel.
He just stood there with his eyes closed. At
last, he waved his umbrella and shouted,
'Now I can go back to India satisfied!' he
called.

Neetu and Sanjay looked at their mother,
puzzled.

'Can Grandpa see lots of things with his
mind's eye?' asked Sanjay.

'I wouldn't be satisfied just seeing it in

my mind,' muttered Neetu. 'He could have stayed at home and imagined it there.' She couldn't help feeling let down. She had thought that Grandpa could never be wrong. She really believed he would find a field of poppies.

'Oh, well,' said Mum kindly. 'Let's go home.'

By the time summer came, Grandpa had gone back to India. He wrote them a letter and said, 'I will never forget the beautiful poppies. Perhaps, next time you go back to the railway tunnel, you can pick one for me and press it in a book and then send it to me.'

'But, Mum, there weren't any poppies!' cried Sanjay, shaking his head.

'He was just imagining things,' snorted

Neetu indignantly.

'Take me to this tunnel. It sounds interesting,' said Dad. 'For once, I feel like a walk.'

'Oh, yes! And this time, can we take our bikes?' begged the children.

'I hope I can remember the way,' murmured Mum. 'Perhaps that black cat will turn up and help us.'

It was a quiet June afternoon. The streets were hushed with an after-lunch sleepiness. The children rode their bikes on the empty pavements. Somehow they easily remembered the way they had walked with Grandpa. They reached the church on the corner. The black cat was sitting on the wall, as if it had been waiting for them all this time. Time wound backwards. Everything

happened in the same way. The cat led them
down the road to the cul-de-sac and then

 leapt up the
path between
the houses.
When they
reached the
steps of the

railway bridge, Mum and Dad carried the
bikes up and over and down the other side.
Once on the track, Neetu and Sanjay
mounted again and went pedalling on
towards the tunnel as fast as they could. This
time, they didn't hesitate when they reached
the black opening of the tunnel, but plunged
inside. Their laughter echoed on and on.

Now Mum and Dad reached the tunnel
entrance. They could see their children's

shapes outlined far ahead in the silvery daylight at the other end.

Suddenly they heard a shriek of astonishment. 'Mum! Dad! Look!'

The parents ran. The children stood still in the darkness of the tunnel, as if not daring to go out.

'What is it?' gasped Dad.

Mum stopped as if transfixed, then slowly, she walked out into the sunlight. 'Poppies!' she exclaimed.

The railway banks, which just two months ago had been nothing but thick, long, wavery green grass, were ablaze with blood-red poppies.

'Is this what Grandpa saw in his mind's

eye?' asked Neetu in amazement.

'It must be,' whispered Mum. 'I told you he had a special eye.'

Sanjay dropped his bicycle to the ground, and for a while they stood in silent amazement. Then Neetu whispered, 'Shall I pick one for Grandpa?'

'Just one,' said Dad. 'Then when we get home, we'll press it inside our encyclopaedia.'

'Yes, we'll do that!' cried Mum with enthusiasm. 'And later, when it has dried, I'll stick it on to some card and we'll send it to Grandpa in India.'

The poppy dried out in the encyclopaedia, but though it

was flattened, it still looked beautiful on its long stem and its whispery leaves, and it was still as red as the day they picked it. Mum carefully stuck the red poppy on to a piece of white card. Inside, she wrote: 'With much love to Grandpa, who took us on a walk and found a field of poppies.'

Then they all signed their names: Mum, Dad, Neetu and Sanjay.

GRANDPA CHATTERJI'S RECIPE
FOR PAKORA, also known in South India as BHAJJA

Ideal as a snack with tea or drinks, or as a starter, or as a meal in itself if mixed with a generous amount of plain yogurt, slightly salted and spiced, and left to stand for a few hours.

Ask a grown-up to make these with you.

Items required:

a large mixing bowl

a large spoon

a wok or

deep frying pan

a slotted spoon

a plate lined with paper towels for soaking excess oil up

a knife and chopping board

Ingredients to serve two:

11g fresh Beysan flour (chick-pea flour or gram flour), which can be bought in packets in most Indian or Pakistani grocery stores

1/4 teaspoon salt

1/4 teaspoon baking powder

1/2 teaspoon Haldi (turmeric powder)

1/4 teaspoon ground ginger

1/4 chilli powder or well-crushed dried chillies

1/2 teaspoon Dhanyia (ground coriander)

1/4 teaspoon cumin seed (or ground jeera, also spelt with a 'z')

Fresh mint or fresh coriander leaves for added flavour

1 onion coarsely chopped

1 large potato diced into small cubes and softened by being cooked on a moderate heat

for five minutes beforehand

Cauliflower and aubergine sliced and chopped into smallish pieces

Enough vegetable cooking oil suitable for deep frying

Preparing the dough:

Place the flour in a mixing bowl and add water gradually, constantly stirring with a large spoon until a smooth batter is formed. Add the chopped and diced vegetables and the spices and mix them thoroughly into the batter. Add the baking powder.

Ask the grown-up to do this bit:
Heat the vegetable oil in the deep frying pan. Bring the oil to boil, then lower the heat slightly. Spoon in the batter-covered vegetables, one spoonful at a time until the

whole pan is bobbing with little pakoras.
Turn them over and over in the boiling fat
until the vegetables are cooked and the
coating is a golden brown. Remove with a
slotted spoon and place on a plate covered
with a paper towel to drain away excess oil.
Continue until all the batter and vegetables
are used up.

Serve the pakoras piping hot with a dish of
yogurt.